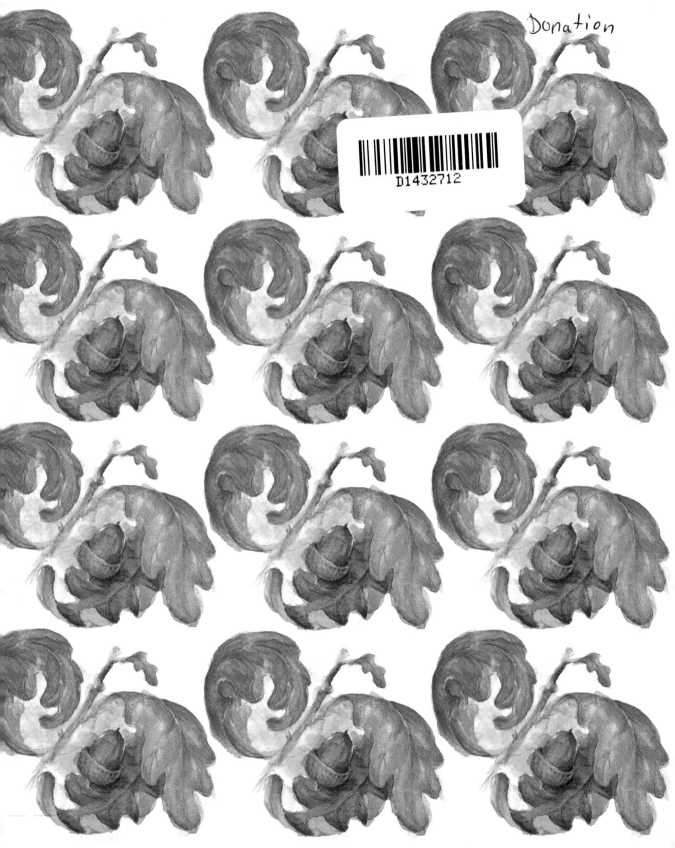

Donation

To Jessica, Francesca and Lizzie

Rabbit

Alison Catley

HUTCHINSON

London Sydney Auckland Johannesburg

Listen, Rabbit

Do you remember spring last year,
When we were telling stories here?

And how when mummy called me home,
You fell, and lay there all alone?

We searched the wood, we searched the park,
We searched and searched till it got dark.
We couldn't find you.

And how next day beneath the tree,
The baby foxes came to see
The funny creature sitting there
With button eyes and tufty hair,
Just waiting.

Long and lonely days went by,
The sun grew bigger in the sky,
And soon the seeds that spring had sown
Had into summer flowers grown.
Poor Rabbit.

But then those foxes came again.
Bigger now, they played a game.

In August, in the morning haze,
You watched the farmer's field ablaze.
While the little mice ran helter-skelter,
Looking for a place to shelter.
Poor things.

The flowers died, the summer passed,
The nights were drawing in so fast.
The tree grew tired, the leaves turned brown.
The squirrels scampered up and down,
Collecting for winter.

Then there came that blustery day
When you were nearly blown away.

Listen Rabbit, I remember
How hard it rained, that September.
You didn't have (it made me cry)
A mackintosh to keep you dry.
I hadn't forgotten you.

And when it *snowed* I couldn't rest
(You didn't have your winter vest).
The snowflakes flew and blew all over
And wrapped you in an icy cover,
While we were warm inside.

But then one fox, now fully grown,
Decided you should be at home.
Do you remember, Rabbit?

Remember how I laughed and cried
To have my rabbit safe inside.
I never will forget, you see,
The day that you came home to me.

First published in 1991 by Hutchinson Children's Books
an imprint of the Random Century Group Ltd
20 Vauxhall Bridge Road, London, SW1V 2SA

Random Century Australia (Pty) Ltd
20 Alfred Street, Milsons Point, Sydney, NSW 2061, Australia

Random Century New Zealand Ltd
PO Box 40-086, Glenfield, Auckland 10, New Zealand

Random Century South Africa (Pty) Ltd
PO Box 337, Bergvlei, 2012, South Africa

Designed by Paul Welti
Printed and bound in Hong Kong

British Library Cataloguing in Publication Data is available

ISBN 0-09-174408-3